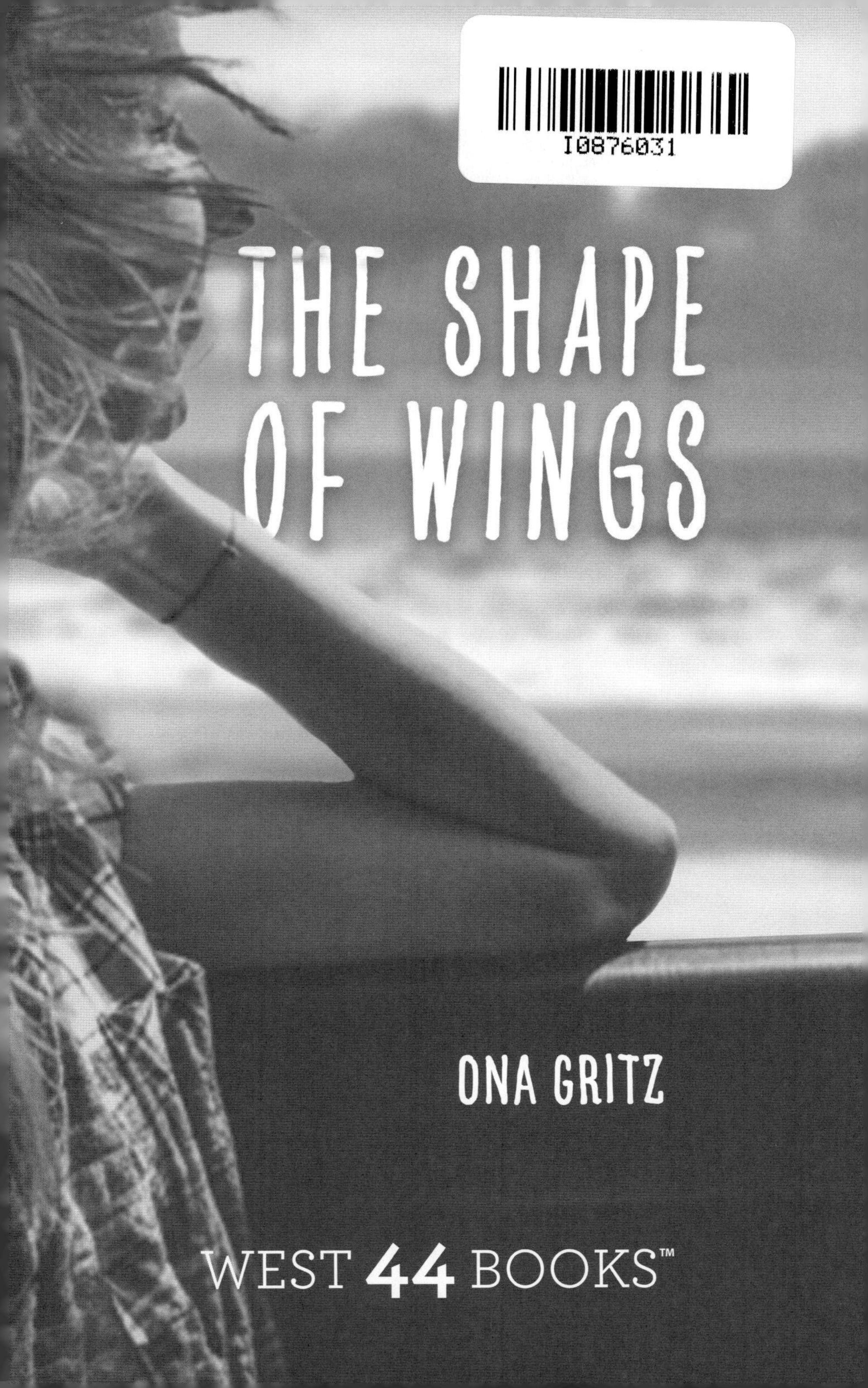

THE SHAPE OF WINGS

ONA GRITZ

WEST 44 BOOKS™

Please visit our website, www.west44books.com.
For a free color catalog of all our high-quality books, call toll free 1-800-398-2504.

Cataloging-in-Publication Data
Names: Gritz, Ona.
Title: The shape of wings / Ona Gritz.
Description: Buffalo, NY : West 44, 2027. | Series: West 44 YA verse
Identifiers: ISBN 9781978598478 (pbk.) | ISBN 9781978598461 (library bound) | ISBN 9781978598485 (ebook)
Subjects: LCSH: Sisters--Fiction. | Cerebral palsy--Fiction. | People with disabilities--Fiction. | Interpersonal relations--Fiction.
Classification: LCC PZ7.1.G758 Sh 2027 | DDC [F]--dc23

First Edition

Published in 2027 by
Enslow Publishing
2544 Clinton Street
Buffalo, NY 14224

Editor: Caitie McAneney
Designer: Tanya Dellaccio Keeney

Photo Credits: Cover (beach) Rudmer Zwerver/Shutterstock.com; cover (girl) Sergey Tinyakov/Shutterstock.com.

Printed in the United States of America

CPSIA compliance information: Batch #CS27W44: For further information contact Enslow Publishing LLC at 1-800-398-2504.

For Dan, my inspiration for Lucas.
My inspiration every day.

And in memory of Harilyn Rousso with endless gratitude and admiration for her creative spirit and life-changing commitment to disabled women and girls.

OTHER BOOKS IN THIS SERIES:

THE SPACE YOU LEFT BEHIND

IN THE WEEKS

since my sisters
and I found
each other,
we've texted.

Shared photos.

Formed a
Red-Haired
Daughters
of Donor #905
WhatsApp group.

Still, it's a shock
to see us all
on a Zoom screen.

Four teenage girls
who look so alike
I almost lose track

of which square
holds me.

WE LAUGH

and I notice
Zoe and Brooklyn
have matching
dimples.

And when
Hannah smiles,
her gums show
like mine.

I like it.
Gaining
an instant
family like this.

Having
a new place
to belong.

BROOKLYN AND HANNAH

both play piano.
Zoe's addicted to
mysteries, like me.

Anyone else a runner? asks Hannah.

Track team! Brooklyn squeals.

While they talk coaches
and meets, Zoe's quiet.

Not a runner either? I ask her.

Gymnast, she says. *You?*

C.C.'s probably into
paddleboarding, Hannah guesses,
since I live by the ocean.

I should tell them I don't
have the balance.
Mention my disability.

But Brooklyn's
moved on to movies.
So I let it go.

I COME OUT

to help set the table.

How was it?
Mom asks.

Hold on, cookie,
Grandma calls
from the kitchen.
Wait 'til I'm
done in here.

Smiling, I lay
napkins and forks
at each place.

I'm pleased
they're curious
about my sisters.

Glad they're
no longer upset
that I searched.

PRIVACY

That's what they
insisted my donor
deserved.
What he
was promised
in those years
before DNA kits
were a thing.

But he's not
who I want
to look for,
I explained
over and over.

Still, they
fought me on it.
Until Grandma
noticed
how I rubbed
my bracelet
whenever we
discussed it.
And understood
before I did
why I craved
knowing my sibs.

THE BRACELET

has two names
engraved on it.
Cara and Celeste.
Mine and my twin's.

Two names for two
red-haired sisters.

One who is now
17.
And one who died
the day we were born.

DURING DINNER

I say it felt weird,
but also good,
to see so much of me
in strangers.

Red curls. Freckles.
How I twirl my hair
when I'm thinking.
Squint when I laugh.

I mention Zoe's
a big mystery fan.
And Hannah
loves Shaboozey,
like me.

When I catch
Grandma glancing
at my hand
on my bracelet,
I notice
what she
must notice too.

I'm still rubbing.
Still missing
the sister
who never
made it here
for me to know.

LATER

I get a text from Paige.
How'd it go?!
my best friend asks.

It was good.
They're all
really nice.
I keep it short,
knowing she's
babysitting.
Tell you more
tomorrow.

She responds
with a smiley emoji.
Texts, *We'll be*
at our usual spot.

My own smile fades.
Perfect, I text back.
Though it's not.

WE

That's the word
that gets to me.

Because these days,
time with my best friend
means time with her
boyfriend, Mike.
And his
best friend, Josh.
And Josh's
boyfriend, Matteo.

They're all my
friends too,
of course.
Still, I miss
having Paige
to myself.

And sometimes
it's hard that we're
an odd number.

Two plus two
plus me.

TO BE FAIR

it was Josh who
encouraged me
to buy the DNA kit.
Back when I was
crushing on him.
Before he came out.
Before he and Matteo
became a thing.

Paige kept the kit
at her house
until I was ready.
Then she and Mike
kept me company
while I spit in the vial
and mailed it in.

Matteo met me
at the library.
Set me up
on Ancestry.
Was there
beside me
when the first
match came in.

THE NEXT AFTERNOON

I spot them
on the crowded beach.
Towels spread
as close to the ocean
as possible without
getting soaked
with the tide.

So? What are they like?
Paige asks
as I join them.

Spill, girl,
Matteo says.

Mike and Josh
stare at me too.
Waiting.

I help myself
to a soda
from Paige's cooler.

I say, *Well, it's not*
like we're identical.
But my bio-dad?
He's got some
really strong genes.

I FILL THEM IN

about Shaboozey.
And mysteries.
Hannah's
gummy smile.
Zoe and Brooklyn
twirling
the red curls
we all share.

That's so wild,
Josh says.

Fantastic,
Matteo agrees,
shaking his head.

But what did it
FEEL like? Paige asks.
Being with them?

I shrug.
Good question.
And I'd try
to uncover
the layers
of my answer.
If she and I
had the time.
And were alone.

AS IT IS

they all have
a volleyball game
to warm up for.

That's right.
They're not just
two couples.
They're
four teammates.

Just one more way
I'm the odd one out.

WHEN THEY LEAVE

to practice punting
the ball,
I lie on my back
in the sun.

Think about
Hannah assuming
a beach girl like me
spends my days
on paddleboards
and Jet Skis.

And about how
I didn't tell her
and the others
I have cerebral palsy.
Didn't explain
that it affects
my balance,
my motor skills
on one side,
my walk.

Instead, I let my
sisters believe
my body's
no different
from theirs.

THE THING IS

I thought I was past
wishing I could
keep it a secret.
I thought I was okay
with my disability by now.

But there's something
about meeting
my sisters.
All of them
into sports.
All of them,
in other ways,
so much like me.

It makes me wonder
what I'd be good at
if I didn't have
cerebral palsy.
Where I'd fit.
Who I'd be.

DAYS LATER

I'm working at the library
checkout desk.
It's been quiet
my whole shift.

I'm deep in the world
of a mystery novel
when I feel a presence.
Look up at a girl
about my age
offering her
library card.

Sorry, I say, taking it.

She laughs. *No worries.*

I zap the card
and her book.
Hand them back.

And that's
when I see it.
The slight
backward curl
of her long
brown fingers.

My palsied hand
does that too.

WATCHING HER LEAVE

I notice
there's a tilt
to her walk.
And without
stopping to think,
I print an extra copy
of her receipt.

My excuse
to follow her out.

JASMINE

I call.
The name
on the receipt
in my hand.

She turns.
Waits.
And as she
watches me,
I'm sure
she's taking in
my slow,
uneven walk.
Recognizing
what it is
we share.

I HOLD OUT

the crumpled
receipt.
Forgot to
give you this,
I say,
my cheeks
heating up
at the lie.

She takes it,
kindly ignoring
the duplicate
tucked like
a bookmark
in her library book.

Thanks, um . . .
She smiles.

And after a
long awkward
pause . . .

I think
to tell her
my name.

SOMEHOW

stammering and shy,
I manage to ask
if we can meet up
for ice cream
at Scoops
when my shift ends
at two.

And somehow,
though I'm no one
to her, a stranger,

Jasmine says yes.
No questions asked.

Not "What for?"
Or "What do you
want from me?"
Or "Why? Because
I walk like you?"

She just shrugs.
Smiles.
Says, *See you
there.*

Leaving me
to ask these things
of myself.

AT SCOOPS

we score a table
on the patio
gated off
from the rest
of the boardwalk.

You live at the shore
year-round?
Jasmine asks.
She eats a spoonful
of her vanilla.
Watches me
carve lines
in my rocky road.

Yup. Just up
the street. You?

New York City.
We come every
summer, though.

Here? But I've never
seen you. I'm sure
I'd have noticed . . . I stop.
Check her reaction.

Yeah, she says
like it's nothing.
I'd have noticed you too.

JASMINE EXPLAINS

how they missed out
on the B&B
where they usually stay
a few towns over.
But I’m only
half listening.
My mind caught
on what we both
just said aloud.

WHAT I NOTICE NOW

is how different
this feels from when
strangers ask,
Are you limping?
Did you hurt your leg?
What happened to you?

Questions that feel
like accusations.
Questions that
translate to
I noticed.

But Jasmine's
I noticed?
Mine?
They translate
to *I see you.*
They translate to
I understand.

AFTER THAT

it feels easy
to talk about
cerebral palsy.
My kind
that splits me
down the middle.
Right side
numb and tight.
Left not affected at all.

And her kind
that stiffens
her fingers
a little, but is
mostly in her legs.
That's why her knees
turn toward each other
when she walks.
Like friends
with a lot to say.

HAVE YOU EVER

met someone new
at a party
while you're sitting?
You're talking
and talking, and then . . .

It's time to stand.
Walk, for the first time,
in front of them . . .

And you see
their face
just change.

Ugh. I know.

HOW ABOUT WHEN

a bunch of people
are sitting on the stairs.

Blocking the railing?

Yup! And when you
ask them to move . . .

They roll their eyes
like you're acting
SO entitled.

Isn't that the worst?

THEN THERE'S

those neighbors who
think they're being nice.
But instead of saying hello . . .

They're like,
"Are you okay, sweetie?"

Right? In that voice
like you're . . .

Only four years old!

AND DON'T FORGET

the ones who
say we're SO brave!

An inspiration!

As if leaving the house
is a feat like skydiving.

"Look at you,
all differently abled."

"Special!"

"Challenged!"

"And yet you let
yourself be seen!"

WE'RE BREATHLESS

and laughing.
Talking fast.
Finishing
each other's
sentences.

And it feels
so amazing
to be so
completely
understood.

Right now,
if someone
were to ask
which one
of us
said what,

I'd say
it's all a blur.

I GLANCE DOWN

and find my
ice cream
all melted.
So I drink it
like a shake.

I've never
talked about
any of this
with anyone, I say.

And it's quick,
but I swear
I see a look
flash across
Jasmine's face.
Like she feels
sorry for me.

YOU DON'T

have one
crip friend?
Jasmine asks.

I think of Alice,
a double amputee
I know.
But she's
closer to
Mom's age
than ours.
More
her friend
than mine.

Jasmine leans
into the table.
You free
tomorrow?
she asks.
There are some
people
you need to meet.

THE NEXT AFTERNOON

I wait on the corner
of Ocean and 9th.
Watch for Jasmine's
space buns and braids.
Her dance of a walk.

A beaten-up
Honda slows
and a round-faced girl,
hair half cropped,
half shaved,
leans
out the driver's
side window.

C. C. she shouts,
pausing between
the letters.
Making my name
yes, yes in Spanish.
Hey girl-Jasmine-met-yesterday.
Come on.

I CLIMB IN

behind Jasmine,
find a guy beside me
in the backseat.
He’s slim, lanky.
Like Timothée Chalamet.
Has his dark curls
and high cheek bones too.

Hey, he says. *I’m Lucas.*
His voice is warm, friendly.

But when I smile
in response,
he doesn’t smile back.

I'M SO GLAD

you're with us,
Jasmine turns
to tell me.
She introduces
our driver, Ysabel.

Welcome, Ysabel says.

We screech forward,
and I notice
Ysabel has only one
hand on the wheel.
Only one hand at all.

We fly down Ocean Avenue.

What's the rush? asks Lucas.

Already told you
I'm late, Ysabel says.

Late for what? I ask.

But we've
hit the Parkway
and the windows
are open.

My voice gets lost
in the wind.

HEY, LEAD FOOT

You're scaring our guest,
Lucas says to Ysabel.
Though I'm pretty sure
only I can hear him.

I laugh. Try
catching his eye.
But he never once
glances my way.

WE TAKE

the exit for
Atlantic Cove,
where, Jasmine
mentioned yesterday,
she's spent all her
summers until now.

It's a fancier
Jersey Shore town
than Sea View.
Fewer T-shirt shops.
More cute cafes.

Finally, we pull
into the lot
of a block-long
building.

What is this place?
I ask.

Jasmine points
to the sign
above the door:
"The Judy Heumann
Activity Center."

Like that's all
I need to know.

LUCAS AND YSABEL

are a couple.
Or at least,
that's what I think
as they walk
around the car
and toward us,
holding hands.

But then Ysabel
pauses beside me.
Places Lucas's
hand in mine.
Breaks into a run.

And Lucas?
He blushes.

Mind walking
with me? he asks.

FINALLY, I GET WHY

Lucas didn't
return
my smiles.
Or my glances.

He's blind.

BEHIND THE BUILDING

There's a strip of beach.
And on it, a volleyball court.
High net stretched wide.
Cones marking corners.
Spectators in beach chairs.
The loud, happy ruckus
of a game underway.

WE FIND

three chairs together.
And I expect
to be bored,
like I'm
always bored
at Paige's games.

And I am at first.

All I see
are fast-moving
bodies.

All I feel
is what
fast-moving
bodies always
make me feel.

Bad about my
own slow self.

BUT THIS

I soon see, is different.

Some of the players
have metal legs.
Some, metal arms.
A few, like Ysabel,
who's playing hard
with them,
are missing hands.

Still, they move quickly.
Keep the ball airborne.

One girl bops it
with her head.
Ysabel lobs it
with a lever
she makes
by clasping
her stump
with the five
fingers she has.

Even though
I don't really
get the rules,
I hoot and cheer
with everyone else.

AFTER THE GAME

Jasmine grabs
Lucas's hand.
Leads us
inside to a gym.
After being in the sun,
the room feels dim.

Players are paired
for what Jasmine calls
volleyball clinic.
But all I see
are awkward
games of catch.

My eyes snag
on kids moving
with the twists
and stiffness
I recognize as
cerebral palsy.

They drop the ball a lot.
Knock into each other.
Remind me
too much of myself.

I THINK OF

something Alice
once described to me.
Sheltered workshops.

They were job sites
for the disabled.
Back when
people assumed
we could only do
the simplest things.

Sort buttons.
Straws.
Marbles.
All for
pennies a day.
Just a way
to feel useful.

This feels
a little like that.
A made-up
fitness center
for the unfit.

JASMINE FINDS

a coach to work with.
Calls me over to join.

I'm good, I say,
embarrassed
by how bad I'd be
even at this.

I stay on the bleachers,
watching and listening.
Learn the kids here
are actually practicing
something called *setting*.
Hitting the ball
in just the right way
so it arcs in the air.

LUCAS CALLS TO ME

Help me practice, C.C.?
He's bouncing a beach ball
with bells inside.

We position
ourselves for catch.

Say something,
so I know
where you are,
he instructs.

I feel silly,
talking just to talk.
Playing with
a toddler's toy.

But Lucas
tells good stories.
Like how the one time
he threw a javelin,
it hit his principal's car.

And for once, it's not
cerebral palsy
causing me
to drop the ball.
It's Lucas
making me laugh.

ON THE RIDE HOME

I'm quiet.
Tired in a good way.
The others are quiet too.

I check my phone.
Find seven messages
from Paige.
All asking where I am.

How would I
describe this day?
Would she even
get it if I tried?

SORRY

I text to Paige.
Stayed late at work.
I'm about to add
See you tomorrow.
But then Jasmine
says it to me.

YSABEL'S HONDA

is outside the library
when I'm done with work.
Like yesterday,
she *yes, yes*'s my name.

I buckle in beside Lucas,
and Jasmine turns
to give me a grin.

We screech
from the curb.
Road trip! Ysabel calls.

Where we headed? I ask her.

Where, you ask? Where?
We're driving just to drive.

FROM MY SPOT

in the back, I watch
Jasmine feed Ysabel
bites of a sandwich.

Tears prick my eyes—
it seems so natural.

Missing a hand?
No worries.
I got you.
No fuss.
No need
to even ask.

WE RIDE

down quiet streets,
past brightly painted
houses.

You drive?
Lucas asks me.

I shake my head no,
then remember
to respond aloud.
I probably could,
physically.
But I get thrown
by all you have to
focus on at once.
And for some reason?
I can't tell how close
other cars are.

You know that's
cerebral palsy, right?
Jasmine turns to say.
Problems with spatial
reasoning.

It is? I stare at her.

Yup. I have it too.

JASMINE ASKS

How's your sense
of direction, C.C.?

Don't have one.

Can you read a map?

Not to save my life.

That's cerebral palsy too.

I gaze out the window,
taking this in.
Feeling . . .
What do I feel?

Relief.

I'm not
stupid like I've
always believed
when I've tried
to decode a map.
Or even follow
a GPS.
I'm just . . .
me.

JASMINE GOES ON

Remember, it's our brains
that are damaged.
Mostly the motor cortex,
which tells muscles
how to move.
But that's next to
the area
controlling sensations.
Hence our numbness.

Hence! Ysabel teases.

Jasmine plans to be
a doctor, Lucas explains.

What's next to
the sensations part?
I ask her.

The area for
spatial awareness, she says.

I shake my head.
And with it,
my fascinating brain.

BIOLOGY CLASS OVER?

Ysabel asks.
She nods to Jasmine.
Plug my phone in.
Pick a playlist.

"Cool for the Summer"
fills the air
with its perfect refrain
about the body
and the mind.

THE NEXT AFTERNOON

after work, Ysabel
picks me up again.

We go back to
the place with the gym.

Inside, I watch
a girl with hemi
cerebral palsy,
like me.
She keeps a volleyball
in the air by palming it
with just one hand.

My first thought:
I could never do that.

My next thought:
Why not try?

I'M EXCELLENT

at dropping the ball.
In fact, I'm perfect at it.
Just like the ball
is perfect at rolling away,
making me chase it.

I nearly die
when I hear
laughter
behind me.
But when I dare
glance around,
no one's
laughing at me.
They're laughing
at their own
runaway balls.

THE COACH

who offers to help me
learn to set
is missing an arm.
So playing one-handed
comes naturally to him.

He has me face a wall.
Says, *Don't slap*
the ball.
Ready yourself for it
using your thumb
and first two fingers.

He demonstrates.
Curling his fingers
on contact.
Opening them
to push the ball away.

Go slow, he advises.
Stand near the wall.
You can step back
and go faster later.
Just get the motions down.

AN HOUR

passes quickly.
By the end,
I've managed
to get the ball
to hit the wall
and meet my hand
four times before
I need to chase it again.

When Jasmine
comes to find me,
I look around
for Lucas.

You won't
find him here,
she tells me.
He never
spends time
in the gym.

WE MEET YSABEL

on the outdoor court
where she's been
practicing with
the serious parasports
athletes.

Lucas is further down
on the beach.
Squeezed beside
another guy,
high up
on a lifeguard chair.

His friend
stares at the sky
through binoculars.
Lucas, head tilted,
is listening.

Are they . . . ?
In this place
a blind lifeguard
seems almost possible.

They're into birds,
Jasmine explains.

I GAZE

at the gulls
circling above us,
and wonder
about the first time
I came here.
When Lucas
spent all afternoon
in the gym.

He claimed
I was helping him.
But now I think
he was thinking of me.
How unsure I
probably felt
about what to do
and where to be.
So he pretended
to need me.

I GLANCE AT THE SIGN

as we pull away.

Who's Judy Heumann? I ask.

Through the rearview,
Ysabel looks shocked.
Only the mother
of disability rights.

Haven't you seen
Crip Camp*, C.C.?*
Jasmine asks.

What's Crip Camp*?*

Best documentary
ever, Jasmine answers.

Movie night!
Ysabel shouts,
honking her horn.

I DIG OUT MY PHONE

Ignore four texts from Paige.
And a long WhatsApp Chat
between my sisters.

*Doing dinner and a movie
with friends,* I text Mom.

Sounds fun, she replies.

I answer with a smiley emoji.
Because it does.

WE ENTER

a big, comfy
beach house.

Towels drying
on the railings.
Sand underfoot.

A girl who looks like
Jasmine but younger
practices flute
at the table.
Two boys who
resemble Ysabel
run through the rooms.
In a loud, crowded
kitchen, adults
laugh and chat
while they cook.

Your families
all live together?

Only in summer,
Jasmine answers,
like it's not
remarkable at all.

YSABEL STARTS THE MOVIE

and a woman's voice
names the colors
and shapes of the logos.
When we come
to footage of two
teenage boys
with a microphone,
she says, *Two*
teenage boys
with a microphone.

Audio description,
Jasmine explains.
For Lucas.

It's distracting, at first.
A narrator telling us
everything we see
as we see it.
But soon, I'm so
in the grip of
Crip Camp,
I hardly
notice anymore.

KIDS ARRIVE

at camp in buses
in footage from 1971.
It's the hippie days.
And the hippies here
are like us. Our age.
Bodies quirky
with disabilities.

I can feel how
thrilled they are
to be together.
And I love how
free and real they are
with each other.

But what
gets me most
is that they're
so ready,
especially Judy,
to change the world.

Make it more
accepting.
More accessible.
And that's
exactly what they
grow up to do.

WHILE YSABEL

drives me home,
she explains how her mom
and Lucas's and Jasmine's
found each other online.
Back when they first
learned their kids
had "special needs."

They formed
a support group
that grew into
a play group
that grew into
summers together.
They even helped start
the Judy Heumann Center.

So for as long as you
can remember, I say.
You've had a Crip Camp
of your own.

AT HOME

that night,
the house feels
too small.
Too quiet.
Too . . .
I'm the only
one
like me.

MOM SAYS SHE'S NEVER

heard of Judy Heumann.
Or the Center.

And when I ask if she
ever sought out other
families with disabled kids,
she says it never
occurred to her.

You always fit in with . . .
She pauses, and I know
she's avoiding
the word "normal."
. . . Paige and your
other friends.

MY RIGHT ARM

does what it does
when I'm tense.
Tightens and folds
like a cooked
chicken wing.

My bracelet
with my sister's name,
which I haven't
messed with for days,
leans on my heart.

What I want to say
to Mom is:
I do and I don't
fit in with them.

AT VOLLEYBALL CLINIC

I'm learning the rules,
and I'm placed on
Jasmine's team.

Don't catch, carry,
or throw the ball,
our coach instructs us.
When it's in reach,
try to hit,
but never twice in a row.

No worries on that one,
I joke. *Not a problem*
I'm likely to have.

AFTER PRACTICE

Jasmine shows me
the holes in the toes
of her sneakers.
They only last a few
months, she says.
Because of my walk.

Same, I say,
and show her
the worn-down
bottoms of my Chucks.

Days later,
spotting a T-shirt
in a boutique window,
we rush inside,
buy two, and change
right there.

Back at the beach house,
Ysabel reads the words
on our shirts aloud.

I may be beautiful,
but I'm awfully
hard on shoes.

THAT WEEKEND

Jasmine, Lucas,
and Ysabel stay home
to catch up on chores.

I decide to finally
catch up with Paige
and the guys.

The first question
they ask, of course, is
Where've you been?

Well, I start.
There's this
activity center
in Atlantic Cove.
For disabled kids . . .

Smart girl, Matteo
interrupts me to say.
Volunteering earns
big points
on college apps.

That's true. Paige nods.
And you've always
been great with kids.

I OPEN

my mouth
to correct them.
But
for some reason,
nothing comes out.

IT HAPPENS AGAIN

that night on Zoom
with my sisters.

Zoe tells us
she's been
practicing
for a big
gymnastics
tournament.

Which gets Brooklyn
excited to share that
she won her race
last week.

So I mention
learning to play
volleyball.

But since I didn't
bring up disability
last time,
I don't know how
to bring it up now.

ON MONDAY

It's a relief
to be back
in Ysabel's Honda
where disability
is a given.
Just part
of who we are.

I read about this
restaurant with all
blind waiters and cooks,
Jasmine tells us.
They keep it dark,
so everyone
experiences eating
without sight.

Love it! Lucas says.

Can we go? I ask.

Jasmine sighs.
It's in England.

Ysabel makes
a screeching U-turn.
You guys give up
way too easily.

YSABEL

squeals to a stop
in the parking lot
of the supermarket.

Lucas, you and I
are on blindfold duty,
she says.
Jasmine and C.C.,
figure out
what we're eating.
Text me when you're done.

We watch them zoom off.
Then we step inside
to a blast of
air conditioning.

Shrugging,
I grab a basket.

I've got a better idea.
Jasmine says.

She leads me to
the electric carts
waiting at their
plug-in stations.

Like dares.

I'VE NEVER

driven anything,
I complain.
Though I'm laughing.
And actually driving.

Jasmine stops her cart
to grab rolls,
and I almost bump
into her.

Then we race to
the freezer aisle,
taking bets
on who will find
the burgers first.

> *Ladies!* a lady
> in an apron yells.
> *Those aren't toys.*
> *And they're not for you.*

Jasmine steps off
her cart,
so I do the same.

> *Oh! No, I'm sorry!*
> Apron Lady
> calls after us,
> watching us limp away.

BLINDFOLDED

we tell the story
over burgers
on the beach house
patio.

You should've
seen her face
when she saw
us walk, I say.
Immediately,
I feel bad,
remembering
Lucas can't see
anyone's face.

But he says,
That's so funny.
And the others talk on.

I notice voices
seem louder
with my eyes covered.
Crickets too.
Also, it's almost
impossible
to get salad onto a fork.
Giving up, I eat it
with my hands.

AFTER DINNER

Jasmine and Ysabel
head inside to hang
with their families.

Lucas stays on the patio,
head tilted.

I stay at the table too.
Slipping my blindfold
back on, I try to hear
what has his attention.

Mockingbird, he says.

It takes me a moment.
But there it is.
Be-de, be-de be-de.
Whe-o, whe-o, whe-o.
Hey you, hey you.

How do you know
it's all the same bird?

Listen, Lucas says.
All those different calls
are from one tree.

I ASK HIM

if he wonders
what birds
look like.
The colors.
The shapes
of their wings.

Do you wonder,
he asks back,
what flying
feels like?

Sometimes . . .

But you don't
spend a lot
of time on it, right?

I GET HIS POINT

No point in wishing
for what can never be.

I start to apologize,
but Lucas changes
the subject.

Describe
the prettiest bird
you've seen.

THE ANSWER

comes quickly.
There's this red one
that visits our yard.
It's small,
but the color
is so bright,
it always
catches my eye.

Male cardinal,
Lucas says.
Now tell me
about red.

IT'S HARD

to describe a color
to someone who's never
seen colors.

I do the best I can.

You know how pine
has a stronger scent
than other trees?
Or how, in some songs,
more instruments
suddenly come in,
brightening the mood?
Red stands out like that.

Lucas lightly
touches my head.
Jasmine told me
your hair's red.

That's true, I say,
sure my face is too.

ON OUR NEXT ZOOM CALL

my sister Zoe asks
how volleyball is going.

I've got
the rotating part down,
I say. *But when*
the ball comes my way,
I tend to duck.

That's just fear,
Hannah says.
You have to
let something hit you.
Something softer.
Do it until
it doesn't
make you flinch.

Rolled up socks?
Zoe suggests.

Or a stuffy,
Brooklyn says.

I grin at my sisters,
knowing just
what to do.
And who to ask.

I NEED TO HEAR YOU

Lucas reminds me.

He's standing
a few feet away,
holding
that bell-filled
beach ball.

I belt out a song
that always
gets Grandma
singing to the radio.
"Hit Me with
your Best Shot."

And,
over and over,
he does.

AT THE NEXT CLINIC

the volleyball
comes
toward me.
And instead
of ducking
out of its way,
I lob it
Ysabel-style.
And the ball
doesn't fall.

It flies.

JASMINE CHEERS

and the whole team
joins in.
Even the players
on the other side
seem pleased for me.
I smile a lot
through the rest
of practice.
And I practice
describing it.
The ball
heading my way.
My body, for once,
knowing what to do.
The ball soaring
like the gulls,
plovers, and terns
Lucas always
listens for.
I practice
describing all this
for him.

EVERY FEW DAYS

Paige texts me.

She and the guys
are going out for tacos.
Or to the movies.
Or the arcade
on the boardwalk.
Would I like to come?

It's great you're
working and
volunteering,
she writes.
But you're
allowed to
have fun too.

I'm just really
busy, I answer,
telling myself
she has the others.
Telling myself
she doesn't need me.

I'M SHELVING BOOKS

at the library
when Ysabel texts.
Wear a suit
tomorrow.

Bathing
Jasmine adds.
Not suit and tie!

I look down
at my jeans.
Dread showing
my uneven legs.

But then I picture
Jasmine.
Her cute
short dresses
revealing
bent knees
and surgery scars.

Be a Jasmine,
I say aloud.

IN THE BASEMENT

of the Center, there's
a swimming pool.

I didn't know this was here,
I say, dipping my toes
in the bright blue water.

Ysabel splashes in.

I can smell the chlorine
from the lobby,
Lucas tells us
as Jasmine guides him
to the steps.

You can smell someone
cooking in Manhattan, she says.

A BLOWUP CHAIR

floats in the pool.
Lucas puts it on
like a hat.

I can't see
with this thing
on my head, he jokes.

I laugh from my place
in the shallow end,
and he turns.
Swims toward me.
Grabs for
my arms and legs.

I LET LUCAS CATCH ME

and pull me under.
When we come up
together,
all I can think is,
Kiss me, kiss me.

And as though
he hears me,
he does.

LUCAS AND I KISS

on the beach house patio.

And up on
the lifeguard chair,
after Lucas
helps me climb.

One time, we start
kissing
in Ysabel's Honda.
When she threatens
to leave us
on the Parkway,
we go back
to just talking
and holding hands.

THE AMUSEMENT PARK

in Rock Beach
has all new rides.

We make the hour drive.
Ride the flume first,
laughing as our log
zooms down
into the water,
soaking our clothes.

For a while,
we split up.
Lucas and Ysabel
to the high, twisting,
turn-you-upside-down
rollercoaster.
Jasmine and I
to the kiddie rides.

Later, Lucas and I
squeeze together
in a capsule
on the Ferris wheel.
So we can kiss
in the sky.

THAT FRIDAY

while I'm at work,
I get a text from Paige.

I have a surprise, C.C.
You have to come
hang with us
after your shift.
Promise?

I start to type excuses
like I've done now
for weeks.
But a wave of guilt
washes over me.

Okay, I say.
See you soon.

I FIND PAIGE

and the guys
in their usual spot
close to the ocean.
Someone else
is there too.

C.C., you remember
my cousin, Jack?
Paige asks.

Jack shines
his bright,
easy smile
right on me.
Paige didn't
tell me
you'd gotten
so pretty.

THE LAST TIME

I saw Jack,
Paige and I were 12.
Jack, at 15, wanted
nothing to do with us.

Once, we convinced him
to play a hand
of Exploding Kittens.
And when Paige
and I made brownies,
he appeared long enough
to eat half the tray.

Mostly, though,
for the few days
he was here,
his eyes were glued
to Fortnite on his phone.
The way, right now,
they're glued to me.

PAIGE HAS ALWAYS

referred to Jack
as *my cute cousin.*
And it's true. Jack's
captain-of-all-the-sports-teams cute.
Underwear-model cute.
Even my mom, a lesbian,
commented on it,
back when he'd only
unglue himself
from Fortnite for baked goods.
That boy will break more
than a few hearts, she'd said.
Not that she worried
about my heart.
Guys like that barely even
see crip girls like me.
Usually.

PAIGE EYES ME

You do look good,
she says.

I wonder if
all the kissing
Lucas and I've
been doing
makes me glow
like in the movies.
Or if my body,
which feels stronger
from all the exercise
I'm getting,
looks better too.

Thanks, I say, blushing.
Not only
at the compliment.
But at everything
Paige doesn't know.

WHILE WE LAZE

in the sun, Jack
talks about Syracuse
where he's studying
computer science.

Matteo keeps
asking questions.
Like he just might
do that too
instead of majoring
in theater at NYU.

I glance at Josh
and he's gazing
at Paige's
"cute cousin" too.
Like we're all
at a museum,
and Jack is the art.

WE HEAD

to the boardwalk
for ice cream at Scoops,
and Jack slows to my pace.

So, C.C., what's up
these days?

It feels wrong
to tell him things
I haven't told Paige.

So I talk about
finding my sisters.
Hanging with them
on Zoom.

Do they look like you?

Definitely.

Four beautiful gingers.
He shakes his head
like the idea
is almost
too much for him.

The way his attention
is almost
too much for me.

I HAVEN'T FORGOTTEN

about Lucas.
In fact, he keeps
popping into my head.
Like it's a room
I've left unlocked.

BUT JACK

slings an arm
over my shoulder
as we stroll
on the boardwalk
with the others.
And I can't help
leaning into it.
This moment.
His touch.
The way
strangers we pass
stare at Jack.
And envy me.

I'M ALMOST

drunk on the feeling
of being chosen
by a guy so many
people would choose.

But, after a while,
I'm also bored.

Jack's favorite subject,
besides how pretty I am,
is Jack.

How he impressed
his programming
professor.
Got picked first
for his fraternity.
How his soccer team
counts on him for the win.

Jack's a hero
in every story he tells.
And he has a lot of stories
to tell.

AND YET

when he offers
to walk me home,
I accept.

And when he
kisses me
under the streetlight
outside my gate,
I let him.

I think I just want to
see it through.
This one day
of being liked
for nothing
but my looks.

The kind of day
I imagine
non-disabled girls
have all the time.

IT WASN'T REAL

In the morning,
that's how I feel
about this thing
with Jack.

It was, of course.
In the sense
that it happened.
But it felt like pretend.

Like I got to live
a few hours
in some It Girl's skin.
Only to discover
I prefer my own.

I'M AT WORK

taping labels
on new paperbacks
when Paige texts.

Ready for another
triple date
after your shift?

Can we meet up?
I text back.
Just you and me?

THE FIRST THING

Paige says is how
happy she is
that Jack and I
hit it off.

There's a concert
tonight on the pier,
she goes on.
Some local band
Matteo likes.
Tomorrow,
we have a game,
and now you won't
have to sit alone.
Jack says he's
psyched to go
with you.

We're on
the boardwalk.
On a bench that
faces the beach.
And I'm glad
to have something
to look at
instead of her face.

JACK'S ATTENTION

was flattering,
I say to the wild waves.

I got caught up in it.
But I shouldn't have.
I can't see him again.

FOR A MOMENT

Paige is quiet
beside me.

A really
brief moment.

I get it, she says.
I know he's only
here a couple
of weeks.
But it doesn't
have to be
serious, right?
Jack will go back
to college.
We'll start
senior year.
But meanwhile,
it's still summer.
And all you've done
is work.

That's not it,
I interrupt to say.
There's someone else.

PAIGE SIGHS

Okay, she says.
So what?
You have a crush?
Jack likes you.
And he's here,
in the flesh.

Paige! I burst,
insulted that
she assumes
I could only
mean something
one-sided.

And it hits me.
That's part of
why I let Jack
get to me yesterday.
Assumptions
like that about
crip girls like me.
Assumptions
I make too.

IT'S NOT JUST

some crush,
I tell Paige.
I'm seeing
someone.
In the flesh.
Someone
I like a lot.

What?
Who?
Where'd you
meet him?
Is it a him?
When?
Is it someone
I've met?

Her questions
keep coming,
leaving no space
for answers.
Until she gets
to the one
I don't know
the answer to.

How come
you're just
telling me this now?

I IMAGINE

telling her everything.
From meeting
Jasmine in the library
to kissing Lucas nonstop.

And that's just how
I imagine telling it.
Nonstop.

But I only get
as far as Ysabel's car
pulling up to the Center
that first afternoon

before Paige
has more
questions to ask.

SHE GRIPS MY ARM

Wait, she says.
That place?
Where you
volunteer?

Yeah, but . . .
I don't actually
volunteer there.

But you said . . .

I didn't.

Sure you did . . .
She pauses
like she's trying
to remember
my exact words.

I said, there's
this center
for disabled kids . . .

Right.

I meant kids
like us.
Our age.
And disabled
like me.

PAIGE LOOKS AT ME

and she looks confused.
Why didn't you just
correct us?

It's a really good question.
And, once again,
when I try to find
the answer,
my mind goes blank.

LET ME JUST

tell it my way, I say.

This time,
I start with Lucas.
How he loves birds.
Looks like
Timothée Chalamet.
Tells really funny stories.
And how, though
he can't see,
he pays close attention
to everything
around him.
Especially me.

I'M STARING OUT

at the ocean again
as I tell Paige all this.
And when I finally
turn to her,
the hurt in her eyes
is enough to make
my own eyes burn.

I can't believe
you met this great guy,
she says, *and kept it*
a secret. From me.

I DON'T KNOW

what to say.
So I don't say anything.
Neither does Paige,
but I can almost
hear her thinking.

She sighs.
Straightens
her shoulders.
Decides, I think,
to find a way past this.
A way in
to my new life.

Turns out, I'm right.
And I love her for it.

Okay, she says.
Tell me how you knew
you wanted to be
more than just friends.

I TELL HER

our first kiss
surprised me and didn't.
It felt so right, I say.

Then I go back
to the beginning.
When Lucas
pretended
to need my help
so I'd feel
more at home
in the gym.

Later, I kept ducking
during volleyball
practice.
So he agreed
to make me
a human target
for a beach ball.
It worked. I got
over my fear.
Actually started
playing
pretty well.
I turn.
Grin at her.

But Paige
isn't smiling at all.

PAIGE'S VOICE IS WOBBLY

I'm trying to decide
what's worse, she says.
That you have these new
friends who mean more
to you than I do.
Or that you didn't tell me
about your boyfriend.
Or that you've been
learning a sport
you've always hated
but I've always loved.
And I'm the last to know.

BEFORE I CAN RESPOND

Paige is off our bench
and running, knowing
I could never catch up to her.

Come on, Paige, please!
I call after her.

But she doesn't slow down.

I TEXT PAIGE

over and over.
I'm sorry, I write.
I know I hurt you.
It was wrong
to leave you out.
No heart emojis.
No prayer hands.
They would just
seem false.
Answer me,
please? I beg.
But my phone
stays silent.
Past dinner.
Past dark.

FINALLY

I hear a ding.
And I feel
like I can
breathe again.
I grab my phone
off the nightstand.
Turn the screen
face up.
But the message
isn't from Paige.

It's three
short words
from Jasmine.
We saw you.

I START TO TEXT

Saw me when?

But I decide
to Facetime instead.

Because, right now,
all I really want to do

is see my friend.

MY PHONE SCREEN FILLS

with two faces.
Jasmine's and Ysabel's.
Heads pressed together.

It's so good to
see you guys, I say.
I haven't had
the best day.

Poor you,
Ysabel responds.

It takes me
a second
to take in
the coldness
in her voice.

What's wrong? I ask,
afraid I already know.

STARING PAST ME

Jasmine says,
Last night,
we went out
for a pizza run.
We thought
it would be fun
to surprise you.
So we drove
to your house.
She pauses.

And Ysabel
jumps in.
You might
have noticed
we were there,
she says.
If you weren't
so busy
making out
with some dude.

I EXHALE

Grateful they're
staying
on the call,
willing to listen.

It was a mistake,
I tell them.
It definitely
didn't mean anything.

I stop.
Wait for them
to say something.

Finally, Jasmine does.
Lucas was there too.

TEARS SPRING TO MY EYES

We didn't
tell him what we saw,
Jasmine goes on.

But before I can feel
relieved by that,
Ysabel adds,
It's not our job
to hurt him for you.

And they end the call.

I SIT FROZEN

on my bed.
Phone clutched
in my fist.
Its screen
staying blank
and dark.
Its silence
stretching
on and on,
saying
everything
there is to say.

THAT NIGHT

I don't sleep.
And in the morning,
I can't eat.
At work, I mess up
everything I touch.
Paste the wrong
labels on books.
Place magazines
out of order
on the shelves.
Misspell the titles
I search for
on the computer.
Until my boss Adela
suggests I go home.

LUCAS TEXTS

Hey, missed you today.
Ysabel said something
about your work
schedule changing.
See you tomorrow?

I START TO TEXT

Hey back,
then erase it.

What can I
possibly say?
That I kissed
someone else?
A guy I don't
even like?

"That's right,"
I imagine him
hearing
in the robot-like
voice that reads
his screen.
"I messed
everything up
for no reason."

I shove my phone
in a drawer.

I WRITE TO MY SISTERS

the next morning
on WhatsApp.
Can't make
our Zoom
meetup today.

Everything okay?
Brooklyn asks.

Just busy, I say.

Busy hurting
everyone I know.

SEE YOU NEXT WEEK

I write. But I'm not
even sure that's true.
If I duck out now,
I never have to
admit to my sisters
that, all this time,
I've been
dishonest with them,
along with everyone else.

I FIND GRANDMA

out in the garden.

What's new, cookie?
she asks.

When I don't answer,
she studies my face.
Nods.
Hands me a spade.

WITHOUT A WORD

I kneel beside her
in the dirt.
We plant zinnias.
All different colors.

It's soothing,
for a while.
Working quietly.
Keeping my
hands busy.

But it hurts too.
Thanks to
the Carolina wren
singing
and singing
over our heads.
A bird
I wouldn't even
know the name of
if it wasn't
for the boy
I'm too
chicken to call.

HEY

Lucas texts again.
Are you okay?
Pause . . .
Are we okay?

You're the best,
I text.
But me?
I'm definitely
the worst.
You deserve
so much better.

Thankfully, he
can't see the dots
that would
let him know
I'm typing.

I don't hit send.

HE CALLS TOO

The first time,
he leaves a message.

Hey, C.C.
I don't know
what's going on,
but would you
call me or text
or something?
I hope you're
all right.

After that,
a few hang ups.
And then finally
nothing.
Just the silence
I deserve.

I WORK LATE

at the library to fill time.
When I get home,
Mom's book group is there.

I nod to her guests,
then slip into the kitchen

Alice follows
in her motorized chair.

I hear you've joined
the Judy Heumann Center,
she says. *I knew Judy.*

Really?
I lean against the counter.
How?

We'd see each other
at protests.

Wow!
I'm excited,
for a moment,
to tell the others.
Then I remember.

I don't have others to tell.

ANYWAY

Alice says.
It's so great
that place exists.
There was nothing
around here
for disabled kids
when I was your age.
You're very lucky,
you know?

Lucky, I repeat,
swallowing past
the lump
in my throat.
I definitely was.

MY RIGHT ARM

has been doing its tight
chicken wing thing.

I've also gone back
to rubbing the names
on my bracelet.
Cara and Celeste.
Mine and my twin's.
Because the thing is,
there were supposed to be
two of us.
I wasn't meant
to figure everything out
on my own.

THE LAST TIME

I felt this alone
was the day I discovered
Celeste had existed.

No secrets, no lies,
Mom and Grandma
had always promised.
Yet they'd kept
Celeste a secret
from me.

Except, my body knew.
I felt her absence.
And it hurt
that I couldn't place
who it was
I missed so much.

How could you
not tell me?
I kept asking,
feeling so betrayed.

Meanwhile,
look at me now.
Keeping secrets.
Telling lies.

THAT NIGHT

I wake, fingers
on my bracelet.
And something
makes me sit up.
Switch on the light.

Oh no, oh no, oh no.

Our names are fading
from all the touching.
The grooves
nearly rubbed out.

Mom! Grandma! I call.

They burst
into my room.
Join me on my bed.

Look what I did,
I say between sobs.
I ruined my bracelet.
Just like I ruin
everything.

GRANDMA ROCKS ME

And Mom studies
my bracelet.
Honey, this is fixable.
We'll just bring it
to a jeweler.
Nothing
to cry about.

But Grandma
knows that isn't
what's causing my tears.
It's okay, she whispers,
holding me tight,
just like she did
when I was little.
Whatever this is,
it'll be okay.

WE

fall asleep like that.
Our posse of three
curled together
in one bed.

Sometime
in the middle
of the night,
I wake.
Feel relieved
they're still there.

The fight about
Celeste comes
back to me again.
How I'd sobbed
and screamed,
really believing
I could never
trust them again.

Yet here we are.

I ACCEPTED

their apologizes.
But it wasn't just
their saying sorry
that let us be us again.
This new version of us
that had been
through something.
It was the going
through it that did it.
The hard talks.
The way they
worked to
understand why
they'd kept
my twin a secret
so I could
understand too.
It was their honesty,
finally.
That's what it took
to make up for the lies.

IN THE MORNING

I text Paige.
And when she
doesn't answer,
I text her again.

I call too,
leaving long
voicemails she
probably won't
listen to.

When I don't
hear back,
I show up
at the house
where she babysits.
I hear the television.
And the kids giggling.
But Paige won't
come to the door.

She texts, though,
while I'm still out
on that stoop.
If I agree to meet,
will you stop
stalking me?

WE'RE BACK

on our bench
at the boardwalk.
Only this time,
I sit sideways.
The metal armrest
digs into my back.
But I make myself
stay there.
Make myself look
directly at Paige
while we talk.

I DON'T GET IT

Her voice
is clogged with
held-back tears.
I never left you
out of anything, C.C.

I know, I say.

I mean, if you
told us you wanted
to play volleyball,
we would have . . .
She stops.
Because the tears
are winning.

I know that too,
I say.

I DIG IN MY PURSE

for a tissue.
Hand Paige the bandana
that had been my
blind dinner blindfold.

Are you ashamed of us?
she asks.

    What? I blurt, startled
    by the question. *No.*

Then, are you ashamed
of your disabled friends?

    I'm not ashamed
    of anyone, I say.
    Except maybe me.

I TAKE A BREATH

Let it out slowly.
Trust that if
I start talking
and stay honest,
I'll be able to
explain myself
to both of us.

But before I can
begin to find words,
Paige starts up again
with questions.

Why did you keep
your friends
and Lucas a secret?
Let us think it was
some volunteer job?

And the shame I felt
a minute ago
is replaced
by a quick hot
flash of anger.

THAT'S PART OF IT

I say. *Right there.*
You all heard the word
"disabled" and thought,
"volunteer job."
Like the only thing
disabled people
could possibly
be good for
is needing help.

But . . . we thought
you were doing
the volunteering.
So obviously . . .

Obviously what? I ask.
I'm the exception?
Because I'm your friend?
Because I'm not
all that disabled?
It's part of who I am,
Paige. If you
look down on anyone
because of their
disability,
it's an insult to me.

PAIGE SEEMS

stunned by my outburst.
I'm stunned too.
Wasn't my goal
to get her
to forgive me?

No, actually.
It was to make up
for my secrets and lies.
With the truth.

WE TURN AWAY

from each other.
And for what feels
like a really long time,
we stare at the waves
that today are more
ripple than crash.

Finally, without
looking at me,
Paige says
the one thing
that tells me
we'll probably
be okay.
That's fair.

I TELL PAIGE

the volunteer thing
wasn't the whole reason
I'd disappeared on her.

I didn't even know
how badly I needed
to talk about disability.
Or that I'd feel so safe
in a place where everyone
was like me that way.
So safe I actually want to
try a sport.
Me!
I guess, for a while at least,
I didn't want to make room
for anything else.

I FEEL HER TENSE UP

beside me.

Ouch, she says.
And there's real pain
in that little word.

Still, I keep going.
You're always
so busy with the guys.
I figured you
wouldn't really miss me.
It's never just us
anymore, anyway.

PAIGE STOPS ME

Wait, she says.
Before that day
with Jack,
you never asked
that just the two of us
meet up.
Was I supposed
to read your mind?

That's fair, I say.
But at least
some of the time?
You were supposed to
want to hang out
with just me.

IT'S EXHAUSTING

Saying
the hardest things.
And hearing them.
So we spend
the next hour
doing something
we've never done
together.
Even though
we've known
each other forever.
We toss a volleyball
back and forth.
Just that.
No teams. No net.
Nothing to separate us.

PAIGE WANTS

to meet Jasmine, Lucas,
and Ysabel.
She wants to watch
the Center's athletes do
what she never knew
was possible
on a volleyball court.

Soon, I tell her, hoping
more than anything
that it's true.

BUT FIRST

there's something else
on my calendar.
My weekly meet-up
with the Red-Haired
Daughters
of Donor #905.
Next stop on my
truth-telling tour?
Zoom.

I CLICK "JOIN MEETING"

and my sisters
are already there,
laughing.
Talking
over each other.

Zoe's the first one
to notice I've appeared.
Hey, C.C.! she calls.

I nod.
Clear my throat.
I have something
to tell you all, I say.

They get so
quiet and still.
I think our
connection
is bad
and they froze.

FINALLY

I tell them
I have
cerebral palsy.
Describe how it
affects my body.
My right arm
tightens as I talk,
as though proving
my words.

All three of them stare.
And I'm sure
they're furious at me
for not telling them
from the beginning.

But then Zoe says,
I was afraid
you were going
to say you're dying.

And Brooklyn asks,
Did I tell you guys
I'm deaf in one ear?

BROOKLYN TELLS US

about the virus
that caused
her hearing loss.

Then Zoe confides
that she struggles
around food.
There's so much
pressure to be thin
in gymnastics, she says.

Brooklyn nods.
My mom was a dancer
and she's gone
through that too.

I don't make myself
throw up or anything,
Zoe goes on.
Just measure what I eat.
But I've gotten better
thanks to group therapy.
It helps to talk
to people going through it.

Right? I say.

I LIKE THIS

How real
we're all being
with each other.

But when I glance
at Hannah
in her little square,
petting her dog,
I realize she hasn't
said a word.

must notice too.
We all go quiet at once.

So, no dark secrets
to share, Hannah?
Zoe asks.

I can share
a not-so-dark one,
Hannah responds.
She looks
at her dog Ruby
instead of at us.
It's kind of about
being your sister.
I'm actually not.

ZOE SAYS

what I'm thinking.
I'm confused.

From the look
on Brooklyn's face,
she's thinking it too.

Are you ditching us?
I ask.

Hannah gives us
a gummy smile.
No way.
What I'm trying
to say is
I'm non-binary.
Still yours.
Just not a her.

HANNAH TELLS US

she, no, *they*
have a new name.
Harper. For their
favorite author.

I only recently
figured this out, they say.
And it makes me
finally make sense.
To me.

I nod.
And I keep nodding.
Because something about
what Harper is saying
feels familiar.
And true for me too.

COMING OUT

You know, I say,
I think I've also
been going through
a kind of coming out.

Say more, Harper prompts.

I used to think disability
was just what was
wrong with me.
But really it's
an identity too.
If you claim it, that is.
And I finally do.

Huh, Brooklyn says.
I guess I do too.

I FIND MOM

reading on the front porch
and plop into the chair
next to hers.

Mom?
Remember when you
told me the best thing
about coming out
was finding
your people?

She glances up
from her book.
I do, she says.
And it was.
Nothing's as lonely
as thinking you're
the only queer person
in Sea View's
giant high school.

I can think of
one thing, I say.

WHAT I HAVE TO TELL HER

is simple.
A simple truth.
She was wrong
when she didn't try
to help me find
my people
when I was little.

You felt
what a difference
it made for you,
I point out.

She nods,
her eyes filling.
You're right, she says.

I nod too,
but my eyes are dry.
I know.

MOM PULLS UP

in front
of the Judy Heumann Center.

This is so close to us,
she says,
shaking her head.

I can tell
she feels guilty.
Good, I think.
She should.
She should have
been among
the founding parents
of this version
of Crip Camp.
I should have
grown up
knowing
kids like me.

I REACH

for my bracelet,
forgetting
it's at the jeweler.

All that's there
right now
is a tan line.
An absence
to mark
an absence.
How painfully
perfect is that?

STILL TOUCHING

my bare wrist,
I turn to Mom.
She's gazing
out the window.
Shoulders
slumped like
she's holding
something heavy.

A hard part of me
peels away,
allowing me
to remember.
The day she
became my mother,
she lost Celeste too.

GRIEF

changes the brain.
Jasmine told me that
on a rainy day
while we watched
a heartbreaking movie
about a widower
who assumed
his life had ended
with his wife's.

Jasmine said
that kind of loss
rewires the brain
for a while.
Makes the mind
foggy.
Pulls words
out of reach.
Causes
the grieving person
to make all kinds
of mistakes.

HAPPY/SAD

We were so happy and sad
at the same time,
Mom told me
the day I learned
of Celeste.

She and Grandma
chose to focus
on the happy part.
Because I
needed them.
And, she'd said,
she never
wanted me to feel
like I wasn't enough.

Now, I place
my hand over hers
on the steering wheel.
Thank you, I say.

Any time, honey,
she responds, thinking
I mean for the ride.

I HEAR IT

before I see it.
The thumps, cheers,
and shouts
of a volleyball game
on the outside court.

I rush past,
not wanting to be seen.
Knowing Jasmine
and Ysabel
don't want to see me.
At least not before
I find Lucas
and try
to make things right.

HE'S THERE

on the lifeguard chair.
Focused on gulls
screeching and wheeling
overhead.

If I call to him,
I'm not sure
he'll hear me.
And his buddy
isn't there to tell him
I'm below.

I take a breath
and slowly
start up the ladder.
Missing
the reassuring feeling
of having him
behind me.
Warm hands
on my waist.
Warm voice
in my ear.
No worries.
I got you, C.C.
I'm here.

THERE'S A MOMENT

at the top rung
when you have to
ungrip your hands,
swing your butt
onto the chair
and face front.

Last time,
Lucas helped me.
This time,
I'm stuck.

I PLACE MY HAND

on his foot.
Watch his face
startle
at my touch.

Lucas?
It's me, C.C.
Help me up?

IN ONE QUICK MOVE

he has me,
strong hands
under my armpits.
He lifts me.
Plunks me down
beside him
on the hard,
splintery chair.

Hi, I choke out.
The only word
I have breath for.
The only word
I can think of to say.

I STUDY

Lucas's face,
and while his eyes
don't show feelings,
his brow tightens.
His cheeks redden.
His Adam's apple
moves like he's
working to swallow
something bitter
in his throat.

Why did you
disappear, C.C.?
he asks.
Who does that?

TAKING HIS HAND

I say, *I did*
something stupid.
And I was afraid
to tell you.
That's why I
stayed away.
Which, of course,
was stupid too.

I TELL HIM ABOUT JACK

How he poured
attention on me
like shaken-up cola.
And how I drank
that too-sweet stuff up
until I felt almost sick.

Lucas tilts his head
like he's listening
to the gulls
that swoop
all around us.
But he's not.
He's listening to me.
Listening is something
he's so good at.
I've missed that
about him.
I've missed
everything.

JACK

brags a lot,
I tell him.
I got bored
with it
pretty quickly.
I never saw him
again after that
one long day.
But . . .
I close my eyes
as I say this.
We kissed.
And I don't even
know why.

LUCAS

shakes his head.
Really? he asks.
Because I'm
pretty sure I do.

I flinch.
like I used to do
in volleyball.
Only now,
it's not so much
my pain
I'm afraid of.
It's his.

HE CAN SEE YOU

Lucas goes on.
So his being into you
said something
you wanted to hear
about how you look.

He's not wrong.
And I almost
hate myself for it.
But there's
more to it than that.

ALL THE BOXES

This isn't an excuse, I start,
feeling my way
toward what I'm
trying to say
as I say it.
Until this summer,
I've lived as an
almost-able-bodied girl.
And there are things
in that world
I've been taught
to want.
And you're right.
One of those things
was a handsome guy
finding me beautiful.
Jack checked that box.
But you?
You check all the others.
The ones that actually count.

LUCAS SIGHS

His version
of rolling his eyes.
You think
I can't tell
you're beautiful?
he asks.

I . . . I'm not sure
what to say to that.
Except to ask*, How?*

I've heard your
voice, C.C.
Touched your hair.
Smelled you after
a sweaty game of
volleyball.

I laugh,
and it feels like
letting out
a long-held breath.
Because it is.

I DON'T EVEN KNOW

who leans in first.
All I know
is how right it feels
to kiss Lucas.

Is it okay, I ask,
if you're the only
person I want to kiss
from now on?

Lucas grins.
I can live with that.

A VOLLEYBALL

lands in my lap.

Hey, Ysabel
shouts up
to Lucas.
That girl
bothering you?

Yup! But I'm
bothering her right back.

He helps me climb down.

Soon, I'm walking
with Jasmine.
You guys talk? she asks.

We did.

She smiles and I notice
an extra bounce
in her already
bouncy walk.

My heart,
which she once
described
as about the size
of my fist,
unfolds like wings.

I'M AT MY DESK

Paige, Jasmine,
Lucas, Ysabel,
Josh, Matteo,
and Mike
are all crowded
around me.
They stare
at my screen
as I click
"Join Meeting."

My red-haired
siblings appear.

Lucas's hand
is in mine.
Jasmine and Paige
each rest a palm
on one of my
shoulders.
My siblings
beam at us
from their squares.

I'm so excited, I say,
for all of you
to finally meet.

IF YOU ENJOYED THIS BOOK, MAKE SURE TO READ THE FIRST BOOK IN C. C.'S SERIES:

THE SPACE YOU LEFT BEHIND
BY ONA GRITZ

ISBN: 9781978597068

Meet C.C.

Paige says to the guys
who've joined us
on our beach blanket.

Mike and Josh
are on my team,
she tells me.

The cute one
grins at me.
He's Josh.

Paige and Mike
start talking
volleyball.

Josh asks what
C.C. stands for.

Cara Carrot, I admit.
My cheeks red.
Even more than my hair.

Josh and I chat about
favorite bands.
Boardwalk movie night.

And—*Oh my God,*
you love it, too?—
the *Everyday*
Mysteries podcast.

Scoops?

Mike cuts in to ask.
That's the best
ice cream stand
on the Jersey Shore.

Josh grins.
Paige gets up
and brushes
sand from her legs.

I gaze at
the ocean waves.
Want to say
I'm feeling too lazy.

Though really,
I'm just not ready
to let Josh see

that when I walk,
I limp.

That always
breaks the spell.

The Friend Zone

That's where guys
move me
once they know
I have
cerebral palsy.

Mom says
that's a good thing.
Then I won't
wind up

with someone
too shallow
to like me
for the right reasons.

Whatever that means.

Take a
Sad Song
Ona Gritz
STEREO
45

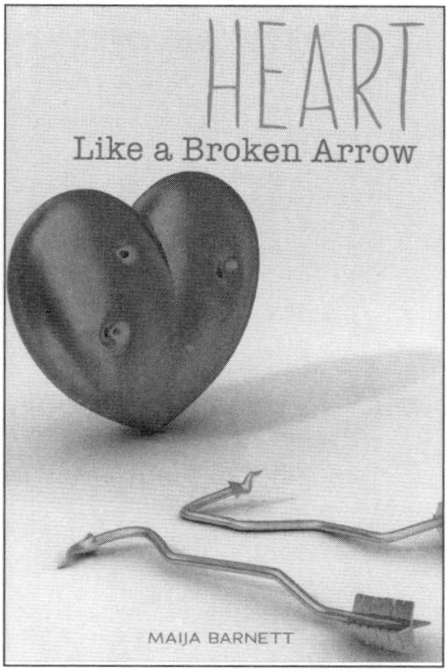
HEART
Like a Broken Arrow
MAIJA BARNETT

THE SONG I'M IN

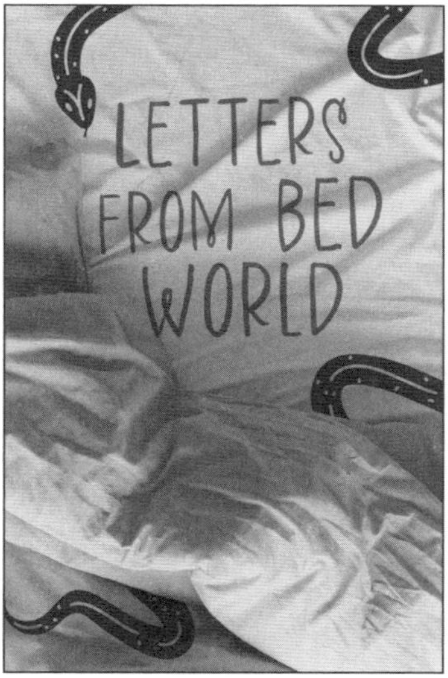
LETTERS
FROM BED
WORLD

ABOUT THE AUTHOR

Ona Gritz holds a Master of Arts in poetry from the creative writing program at New York University. She is the author of many books, including the West 44 YA verse novels *Take a Sad Song*, a Kirkus Reviews Best YA Historical Novel of 2024, and *The Space You Left Behind*, an earlier story about C.C. and her friends. Her memoir, *Everywhere I Look* won the Clara Johnson Award in Women's Literature, the Pencraft Best Book Award in Nonfiction, the Readers Choice Gold Award for Best Adult Book, and was named the Storytrade Nonfiction Book of the Year. Find out more about Ona's work at onagritz.com.